ARON BEAUREGARD'S
MORBID CURIOSITIES

BOOK 1:
CAME WITH THE FRAME

Copyright © 2023 Aron Beauregard

All rights reserved.

ISBN: 9798387825507

Cover Art by Luke Spooner

Interior Art by Anton Rosovsky

Cover wrap design by Aron Beauregard

Edited by Kristopher Triana

Printed in the USA

WARNING:
This book contains scenes and subject matter that are disgusting and disturbing; easily offended people are not the intended audience.

JOIN MY MAGGOT MAILING LIST NOW FOR EXCLUSIVE OFFERS AND UPDATES BY EMAILING:
AronBeauregardHorror@gmail.com

FOR SIGNED BOOKS, MERCHANDISE, AND EXCLUSIVE ITEMS VISIT:

www.ABHorror.com

For Rod Serling.

You sparked the imaginations of countless generations and created a ripple effect that will never lose its momentum.

ARON BEAUREGARD'S
MORBID CURIOSITIES

BOOK 1:
CAME WITH THE FRAME

"There is a fifth dimension beyond that which is known to man... a dimension as vast as space and as timeless as infinity. It is the middle ground between light and shadow, between science and superstition, and it lies between the pit of man's fears and the summit of his knowledge. This is the dimension of imagination."

- Rod Serling

CAME WITH THE FRAME

Sophia Couture sifted through the countless tables of odds and ends. She loved a good yard sale. Never being sure what she might come across kept her constantly enthralled. Records, magazines, furniture, books, toys, clothing—the offbeat shots of nostalgia had been flaring up in her brain ever since she had driven past the old Victorian house a few months prior.

Surely, she won't be here this weekend? Sophia had thought. *What are the odds?*

The question had lingered in her head, but weekend after weekend, somehow the woman never ran out of items. It was like she was running a never-ending yard sale. Either that or she was a hardcore hoarder.

Sophia had always been intrigued by what she'd seen from afar—the images of the sale never seemed to leave her mind. Every time she drove down the road, it called to her. The space offered the kind of retro junk that stirred her emotions. It was a shame she hadn't been able to pop in, but the damn timing was just never right—until today.

It didn't take long for Sophia to be wowed. When she saw the picture frame's inky exterior and its bizarrely sculpted dimensions, her jaw nearly fell off.

It's just like Franco… dark, she thought, instantly knowing she *must* have it.

She lifted the frame off the table, feeling its weight. She held it steady and fixed her eyes upon the placeholder photo inside. A mysterious woman that sat by herself in a dark, bland room, a lone light source above only partially illuminating her. An orb peeked out from the background, planetary in appearance. The imagery was far more artistic than any stock photo she'd seen.

It was a typical size. The dimensions and measurements of the frame were printed at the bottom like any other sample image, but still, something about the piece felt different. Maybe the strangest thing about the style choice was that the woman in the snap had her back to the camera—highly unorthodox for what should've been a simple stock photo.

"Weird," Sophia whispered.

"That's an old one," the woman behind the table remarked.

Sophia pointed to the eerie image of the model in the darkened room. "Really? But it still looks like there's a stock photo inside."

The woman shrugged and offered a charming grin. Her face showed her age, but past her wrinkles, there was still something strikingly beautiful about her. An intriguing exoticness captured in her unplaceable accent. The red shawl wrapped around her body was speckled with crescent moons and golden stars that twinkled as bright as her eyes. The woman didn't say anything more, she just continued to look around at the potential clients perusing her tables.

Sophia figured the woman was just the type to say whatever the customer wanted to hear to close a sale. An item's age at an antique store or yard sale was always a point of enticement. Sophia wasn't so much concerned about the history of the frame—she just wanted to secure it.

She looked down at the ebony rectangle. "Regardless, it's beautiful. How much are you looking for?"

The wrinkly woman's expression fell flat as she took a moment to ponder. "I can do five."

Sophia's eyes popped—she was scoring a deal. She reached into her purse and plucked a Lincoln from the cash wad buried inside.

"I'm so glad I was able to stop in," Sophia said. "I've seen you out here a few times now, but the stars never aligned." She reached out with the money while looking from her shawl to her eyes.

"It seems this frame has been waiting for you," the woman replied.

Sophia smiled politely. "Really? What makes you say that?"

The woman took the money from Sophia's hand. "The stars tell us many things. Even when we can't see them, they speak to us."

Sophia was intrigued by the woman's odd way with words. She spoke like a palm reader laying out cards in front of a crystal ball. A fun attraction that she might've sought out in her twenties. The transaction had been completed but she felt the need to ask another question. "And what do they say to you?"

She slipped the money into a steel black box beside the table. "They say that some of us need help and don't even realize it. They tell me that this frame, it's not for you." She looked down at Sophia's hands and at the sharp teeth of the gargoyle and demon faces imbedded in the frame's charcoal perimeter. "Surely such a dark, daunting piece couldn't align with your aura, could it?"

Sophia furrowed her brow, not exactly sure of what she was getting at. "I—I wanted to give it to my boyfriend. He's a photographer. He loves unique frames."

The woman nodded subtly. "Well, it does have a lot of character."

Suddenly, a slight snarl of annoyance crept up on Sophia's face. Her mental state shifted from thinking about the woman and her items to the man in her life.

"All of *his* frames are currently occupied, but it's not with pictures of us," Sophia quipped.

The woman's eyes widened with disbelief. "How dreadful of him."

"I know!" Sophia said. "It must sound crazy, but it's always all about his work. But this one," she tapped her fingernails against the glass and winked, "is coming with a stipulation."

The woman adjusted her shawl and bobbed her head in approval. "That's perfect, dear. I'm sure he'll appreciate you after this. I know I would."

She grinned at Sophia, her lips parting to reveal a collection of rotten teeth that shared the same tone as the frame she'd just unloaded.

A PARTING GIFT

Francisco Booth looked up at the curious photograph in the glass frame surrounded by a wavy garish trim. The woman portrayed in the stunning image lay partially nude on a shaggy rug. Fright bled from her pupils and her cheeks were discolored—slickened with several streaks that were a combination of mascara and teardrops.

A stark look of disappointment clung to his face. Something about the photograph bothered him deeply. Huffing, he looked away from the wall and over at the bookcase. Many of his photography albums, amongst other books, sat shelved. He keyed in on the raven candle holder affixed to the wall beside the case. As he took a step closer to it, he muttered, "Got to be smart."

Franco reached up for the long cylinder that rested above the stone bird's head, but just before he made contact with the candle, his train of thought was interrupted.

"You're smart enough," Sophia said.

Her voice surprised him. He wasn't expecting to hear it again for some time. Franco immediately twisted around, agitation attached to his eyes. "Christ, you scared the shit out of me! What—aren't you supposed to be on a plane right now?"

"I didn't mean to startle you, but that *is* part of surprising someone, I suppose. My flight didn't leave at noon, I kinda fibbed."

Sophia stood holding a unique ebony frame in one hand and a white envelope in the other. Her cute little curl of the lips was so sweet and warm it was challenging for Franco to stay mad at her. He let go of his outrage.

"Surprise?" he asked. "What have I done to deserve this?"

She smiled. "How about just existing? Oh, and loving a nerd like me is bonus points."

Franco knew she was right. Sophia was dorky and rather ordinary. But that might've been what drew him to her. Outside of work, he needed someone that wasn't carved out of perfection. The majority of the girls that graced his lens were a handful—conceded, careless and condescending. Sophia was refreshing. She helped him detach from the vanity and politicking that regularly plagued the profession he'd chosen. But more than any of that, she made him feel. She triggered emotions he'd never known he was capable of until she'd entered his life.

"Wow, that's a really interesting frame," Franco said, finally taking notice of the beautiful outline.

"It's all yours." When Franco tried to reach out for the frame, Sophia jerked it back quickly and continued, "Under one condition, that is."

Franco raised his eyebrows reluctantly, wondering what she was cooking up. He didn't want to ask but he was going to find out one way or another. "Okay, I'll bite."

Sophia looked around the elegant space, a scowl of discontent curling her lip. "You must have at least fifty frames hung in this house, but not a single picture of us. I know photography is what you love, but what about *our* love? So, since it's clearly not gonna happen without my assistance, I took the liberty of having some of our greatest hits printed for you. All you've gotta do is pick your favorite and pop it inside."

Franco laughed. "Awe, sweetie, I'm sorry. You know how I kinda get wrapped up in my work. I guess I just never noticed."

"Well, I've been living here for over four months now, and *I* have."

"You're so cute when you're mad," he said, pulling her close and placing his lips gently against hers.

Sophia slipped her tongue inside his mouth. After a few seconds of face-sucking, she pushed against his chest. Stunting their embrace, she handed him the frame and envelope. Despite feeling aroused and flustered, Sophia managed to stand her ground.

"Pick one, mister," she said. "Have it done and hung by the time I get back from the conference this weekend. Then there'll be plenty of time to make-out. Now I really do have a flight to catch. I'll call you when I get there!"

"Oh... okay? Have a safe—"

Franco's words were interrupted by her final peck on the cheek. Then Sophia headed for the door and yelled out a parting, "I love you, babe!"

IDLE HANDS NO MORE

Franco sat on the couch in front of the television, staring at Bill Clinton's concerned face. Even though it was months old, they'd been replaying the uncomfortable apology on many stations without fail.

"Shoulda just made her swallow it," Franco grumbled. In some ways, he related to the man. They both had secrets—everyone does.

His eyes drifted away from the political fodder to the frame and envelope full of photos spilled over the coffee table. A mash-up of the wonderful times they'd shared since he and Sophia had crossed paths.

Stop thinking about it, Franco thought.

He looked at the vintage frame, trying to occupy his brain with something that worked. Anything to keep his mind distracted and docile. While the creepy room, dangling bulb, and strange sphere that served as the backdrop of the odd stock image were bland and boring, the woman was anything but. Her wild blonde hair nearly leapt out of the photo. Even though he couldn't see her face, the outline of her body was clearly athletic and toned. The side view of her tight shirt emphasized her aroused areolas—even more so than he recalled when initially looking at the snap.

"God damn," he whispered.

Despite the woman's mystery, there was something about her. He couldn't even see her face, yet she was sexier than anyone he'd ever worked with—which was saying a lot. But at the same time, the woman generated this beautiful feeling in his belly, the same as Sophia gave him.

Or was it better?

The fact that he was even asking was bizarre. Franco examined the stock photo closer. Strangely, while it did display the frame dimensions, it didn't have any company trademarks or branding that he would've expected.

Franco traced his finger over the glass just beside the gorgeous woman. "I wish I could just keep you in here," he whispered to her. "I don't wanna break your heart, but I've gotta move on."

Franco sifted through the numerous photos until he found one of them on the shores of a beach. He didn't put much thought into it but hoped she'd be pleased with the selection. Franco extracted the stock photo from the frame and dropped it into the trashcan. Replacing the vacant space, he slid the sunny snap in and closed the backside.

He put the frame on the coffee table, and his eyes drifted to a photo of another pale but attractive woman that hung on the wall. She stood between a gravestone and a brittle tree with a generous amount of black lipstick applied to her frown. The foliage on the ground was as dead as the look encapsulated in her pupils.

No. I mustn't! Franco thought, fighting with himself. *I've got a lot of things that I need to do here. I've gotta get those new pictures from the Borgia project developed. I can't just allow myself to fall further behind.*

He listened to the echo chamber of fears flutter in his head. A streamline of manufactured ramblings attempting to discourage the compulsions that seduced him. But his desire still burned—a giant black mass bubbling inside him, expanding through every inch of his haunted husk.

Franco never bowed to his fears.

Ultimately, the argument in his head did little to dissuade him. Suddenly, he was wearing his jacket, and his camera bag was slung over his shoulder.

LATE-NIGHT EXPRESSION

"How much further is it?" the woman in the passenger seat asked. "I can't spend all night on one client you know." She pulled at the tight leather skirt and looked down at her drooping top.

"We're almost there," Franco said, "it's literally three streets down. Anyhow—what was your name again?"

"Cassie."

"Anyhow, Cassie, I told you already, I'm gonna make this worth your while. Remember?"

"Yeah, I've heard that before. Problem is, my idea of 'worth your while' ain't in the same ballpark of any john I ever met."

"Well, that isn't the case tonight, okay?"

"If you say so."

Franco peered over at her. It was like a ball of tension was occupying the passenger seat. The woman looked awkward. It was almost as if she didn't know how to unwind. Stress was her only fuel and the tank was always topped off.

"Your eyes," Franco said, "they're incredible."

Cassie looked over, a bit surprised by the comment—she wasn't accustomed to them.

"You think so?" she asked.

"I know so." His tone held the gravest certainty. "They're so bright. They just about glow."

Cassie didn't respond. Instead, she reached into her purse and pulled out a bent cigarette.

"No!" Franco said. "No smoking in the car."

A scowl crinkled her attractive but weathered face as she dropped the tobacco stick back into the bag.

"Besides, we're here."

The side of the brick building had faded graphics on it from when greeting cards were produced there years ago. Since then, it had been turned into a handful of studios for rent, most of which remained vacant due to the downtrodden atmosphere of the location. The grimy nature that region of the city was known for didn't appeal to most in his social grapevine. Many of the girls Franco worked with seemed sketched out when he explained where his photography studio was.

But he was Francisco Booth. His award-winning pedigree afforded him enough clout to influence their perception. He made the grittiest studio feel like a field of fucking flowers. This was a place that thumped with raw human emotion, a space of pain and harsh reality that any *real* artist would be grateful to grace.

Franco parked in the barren lot behind the building. They exited the vehicle. He unlocked the cold steel door that was rusting at the rear of the structure and ushered Cassie down the stairwell until they arrived at the studio's entrance. Once he'd obstructed the keypad from her view, Franco punched in the access code.

"Right this way," he said, grinning as he flipped on the light switch.

"Damn, it's a lot nicer on the inside," Cassie said, making her way to a small table on the edge of the shooting set. She put down her hot pink handbag and took a gander at the surroundings, studying the finely painted walls and fancy equipment within the space.

She also studied Franco. Something about him wasn't quite right. He didn't act like he was preparing for a shoot. He seemed spaced out, daydreaming.

Franco stared at the film-caliber lights strategically placed around the black backdrop. The dark vinyl sheet began at the top of the ceiling and hung down so low that it draped over part of the floor.

Franco walked slowly around the area, activating each of the three lights within the shooting space.

Suddenly, it looked like Franco was in front of a shooting star. Cassie's jaw subconsciously unhinged.

Franco stood behind the tallest light source, the heat from the bulb warming his face.

They didn't take long to get hot.

They didn't take long to mesmerize him.

He spoke quietly. "The glow."

"What about it?" Cassie asked.

Franco didn't answer her. He just continued to feel the heat caress his stubbly face.

"Hello?" Cassie asked, snapping her fingers. "Whatever, man, just give me my money so we can get on with this."

"You'll get your money when the job's done. Now go stand in front of the lights."

"I don't work before I get paid."

"Quite frankly, I don't give a good fuck about how *you* work. I'm the artist, do you understand me?"

Cassie fell silent, used to men talking to her in that fashion.

"Suddenly gone deaf, have you?" Franco asked.

"No, but—"

"Well then, let me snap a few pictures, and this'll be the easiest five-hundred dollars you've ever made. Or, on the other hand, you can walk your smelly ass back to Broadway, and spread your legs long enough to make up for lost time. It's your decision, Cassie, but choosing between a gamut of dirty dicks and a few photos shouldn't be hard. Unless you're a bug chaser or a retard."

Her expression showed how little she enjoyed his comment, but in subduing her emotions, it also showed how desperate she was.

"You better not fuck me," she threatened.

"I know it may seem difficult to accept and understand to someone in such a cynical orbit, but my intention isn't to fuck you. Trust me, I wouldn't dream of it."

A look of disgust crept across Franco's face as he stared at Cassie. She remained scowling, and yet she obeyed.

"Now go stand in front of the backdrop," Franco ordered.

She took a few steps backward.

"Turn around," he said, reaching into his camera backpack on the floor. "I want to begin with a backshot. As if you were just walking down another dark street and someone was watching you from behind."

"Like this?" Cassie asked, facing the backdrop.

"That's pretty good, but maybe try putting one of your hands inside your jacket? Just let it hang there," he directed, unzipping his bag.

Cassie reached deep into her side pocket. "Like—like this you mean?"

Franco reached into the sack and extracted a steel tripod. "Just like that, that's perfect."

Cassie let out a tiny yelp and jumped. The hairs on the back of her neck stood straight. There wasn't anything particularly odd about what Franco had said to her, but the proximity of his voice seemed like he was directly behind her. A place that, based on his prior articulations, he had no reason to be.

Her instinctual reaction was to whip around as fast as she could, but as she turned, the tripod's unforgiving metal met with the side of her face.

A sizable gash left nothing to the imagination, her face now held a new doorway into her flesh. The mushy red meat had been exposed, and a micro-reservoir of ruby drizzle was unleashed from the gash in her skin.

Cassie's disorientation caused her to trip over the excess backdrop piled beside her. As she tumbled, her cranium cracked against the concrete wall that had been obstructed by the backdrop. Stunned, Cassie lay on her side. Confusion swirled in her throbbing skull—she still didn't understand what was happening.

Franco wrapped his fingers around one of the bottom feet of his tripod and twisted. The cap at the bottom was decorative, but it was merely a masquerade for the prick of malice hiding underneath. The murky metallic tip he unveiled was sharper than the point of a protractor and about fifty times the size. As he angled it above Cassie's head, his focus was paramount.

"Not the eyes," Franco whispered.

He lunged downward, going for the gaping wound in her oozing cheek. The lethal tip of the pod punched through the nasty wound on her face, expanding the laceration and pushing deeper until it penetrated the unharmed half. An expulsion of blood and several teeth exited as Franco pulled the point back and angled the leg of the stand out of her mouth.

When the approach changed, the sharp tip scraped over her gumline and carved into the enamel on the left side of her jaw. Franco eventually got the leg exactly where he wanted it—skewering through the side of her face and sticking out of her mouth. Her lips sat around the steel like she was giving a backward blowjob.

Franco was completely tuned out of the horrific gags and body tremors rattling from Cassie. It was simply another day at the office.

"There we are," Franco whispered.

He adjusted his hands so that they were at the top and bottom of the bloody limb of the tripod. The leg was positioned like an enormous oral piercing. He applied harsh pressure to the area of skin and lip tissue that connected over Cassie's jaws. Beneath the human rubber were the leg of the camera stand and Franco's hands.

CAME WITH THE FRAME

He slowly pulled until Cassie's head elevated off the floor, looked into her shock-stained eyes, and lifted his foot with a grin.

"Okay," he said, "so maybe it's not the *easiest* five-hundred you ever made."

As he stomped, Franco's heel landed on her neck, causing the tripod leg impaling her face to pull upward. He was surprised at how easily Cassie's flesh came undone. The expedited way it separated allowed a ghoulish glimpse into the side of her mouth.

Her crimson-tarnished teeth and tarry cavities were now visible. What looked like two pieces of shredded cloth flopped around the upper and lower part of her face as her head whipped backward. The tongue was more intimately visible than Franco imagined it could be, and the side of her face was a hellish curtain of meat.

"Kind of sick when you see how the sausage is made," Franco said, staring down at Cassie with a blank expression.

She attempted to find words despite the destruction visited upon her face. Her mutilated jaw flapped, but as the long, garnet-glazed spike of Franco's tripod came down snugly into her brain, there wasn't anything left to say.

HONEST ART

Franco approached the candle holder that held the raven's outline beside his bookshelf. It had been a day since he'd picked up Cassie—thoughts of her alone were no longer enough. With the care of a newborn, he gently held the new frame under his arm. Fiddling in his pocket, he extracted a keyring from his pants. Twisting it about, he finally located a tiny silver key, then carefully leaned his new frame up against the wall.

Franco plucked the candle from its holder and angled the mini-key downward, feeling around with it. A moment later, the metallic teeth found their groove and it slipped into the unnoticeable hole atop the fixture. He twisted counterclockwise and heard a mechanical hum emanate from the bookcase.

As the shifting shelves slid sideways, they revealed an otherwise hidden dead space within the house. Franco lifted the frame back off the ground and set the candle back where it stood just moments prior. The room in front of him was as black as his heart. Just as Franco finished watching the bookcase open, a thought came to him. *Sure, it's cliché, but too cliché to even truly entertain the notion.*

He grinned devilishly.

Paranoid about being found out, Franco remained in a state of constant assessment. In his mind, there were always things he could be doing better.

If I want to build a legacy, there can be no mistakes...

His paranoia levels had surged even higher after Sophia's little 'surprise' nearly ruined him. Even thinking about the idea was frightening. What would he have done had she stumbled upon his secrets? Would she have ended up hanging on the wall next, another piece within his army of atrocities?

He flipped the switch and a flood of dark red light illuminated the tight room. *No, not Sophia, she's different...* Franco raised the new frame and set it on the fresh hook that awaited it. *We're too much alike, I could never hurt her. Even if I had to.*

As he gazed into the frame and reflected on his most recent ghoulish rendition, Franco couldn't help but feel exhilarated. The tripod stood by itself, blending into the blackness of the background. Cassie's mangled head—or what was left of it—sat atop the vintage-style camera like a protective casing. The destroyed oral flesh blanketed the lens and accessories and the flash attachment peeked out of her ruined mouth from deep inside.

Cassie's eyes had been pulled out, leaving a disgusting pair of deep orbital chasms. Franco had filled them with thin portable flashlights from his bag. They were active and shining bright, and just like he'd told her when they initially met, she glowed.

Despite the spectacle before him, he still couldn't get Sophia out of his head. *But does* this *hurt her?* he wondered, moving on to the photograph beside Cassie's.

The next frame captured an even younger lifeless body propped up in a chair behind the same backdrop. A plum-size circular section of the girl's forehead had been drilled and scooped out, the void filled with a long camera lens that projected out of her skull, the glass eye at the end of the camera symbolizing her forced clairvoyance.

Ashley, he thought, slowly stroking the frame with adoration. *You'll always be my first.*

The morbid art before Franco held a special place in the origin of his evils. So did Sophia. He was a difficult match but she was perfect for him.

She made him better.

She made him normal.

She made him acceptable—at least on the outside.

What she doesn't know won't hurt her.

Franco took a deep breath and soaked in the collection of morbid visions that he'd brought to death on his walls. Standing in the small trophy room gave him a sense of accomplishment.

While it pained him that his most honest and intimate art could never be seen in the light, he took comfort in knowing that, someday, when his heart stopped beating and the house came into possession of a new owner, the world would have no choice but to acknowledge him.

Franco deactivated the lights and stepped through the opening as the bookcase glided shut. The philosophical thoughts died to a simmer inside him as the frame Sophia gifted him suddenly caught his eye.

As a man who paid attention to the details, Franco was mesmerized. The photo of the beautiful day he and Sophia had spent on the beach was no longer behind the glass of the eerie frame. Instead, the sexy woman from the stock photo had once again returned. While her attire was slightly different, he could've certainly picked that gorgeous figure and shimmering blonde hair out of any line-up.

She was special.

But in an inexplicable transition, she was now standing against a dirty brick wall in a scummy alley. An area that she looked painfully out of place at. Still, the filth-caked, green dumpster parked beside her and the wilting cardboard box did little to taint her unmistakable beauty. Her cool blue eyes were hypnotic. Despite the miserable atmosphere, the girl's stunning features still glowed, captivating him with ease.

What the fuck?

He hadn't paid much attention due to most of his focus being poured into his depraved arts, but *he* certainly hadn't swapped out the picture.

"How can it be?" he said. "It—It can't..."

He immediately felt naked.

Like he was being watched.

Like he was being fucked with.

"Hello?" he called out.

No answer.

He rushed, looking around the room before searching the entire house. Nothing was out of order. No windows open, no doors ajar, no gates unlocked. The security system remained untriggered.

When Franco returned to his study, he approached the coffee table and frame for a closer look. The beach snap lay on top of the envelope filled with other photos and his eyes hadn't lied. The woman in the filthy alley remained in frame, confronting him.

Maybe there was another stock photo behind it? Must've just slipped out or something. Yeah, I must've just missed it, and somehow it slipped out.

No matter how he sliced the idea, he couldn't make sense of it. As Franco opened the back of the frame, he extracted the inner-city stock photo and replaced it with the beach shot.

But if that's the case, then the other photo would still be in the trash, where I left it...

Franco didn't mind lying to everyone else in his life, but to himself? There was something about the entire situation that gave him the creeps. He didn't like things he couldn't explain. He was supposed to be creating mysteries, not solving them. The feeling gnawing inside him was what he hated most—not being in control.

It was part of the reason he killed women.

It was part of the very fabric of his being.

I have to look...

Franco rose from the sofa and took a few steps toward the trashcan. He kept his eyes closed because he didn't want to see it. Even outside of the control factor, the recent aura left a weirdness worming through his guts, a foul, solidified certainty that there was no rational explanation for what was happening.

When he found the courage to force open his eyelids, what he could've only registered as a hallucination became reality. The trashcan liner laid forlorn, as bare as the day it was pulled from the box.

ESCAPING UNEASINESS

Franco needed to get out of the house. He hadn't been able to sleep much, knowing that something was off. The unanswerable questions raced through his mind until the sun finally crept through the slices between the curtains of his bedroom window.

I gotta get up. Need to get out of this place, his worried mind thought.

He entered the bathroom and promptly locked the door behind him, something he'd never done before. Upon twisting the faucet, he checked the water to ensure it was warm enough and quickly slid behind the shower curtain. As the hot streams of water massaged his scalp, a disturbing notion continued to reverberate in Franco's skull, one that created discomfort in his heart and fueled panic in his psyche.

Franco hadn't the faintest clue as to what might've transpired in his study the prior evening, but he knew whatever it was, he hated it. Everything felt out of order now. He wouldn't be able to rest until his safety nest was once again galvanized—until he figured out what in the world was going on. He needed to solve the riddle at once but didn't know where to start.

He was almost positive he'd thrown the stock photo in the trash and replaced it in the frame. But since he wasn't really thinking about such a routine and pointless task at the time, it was possible that he might've misremembered the sequence.

Definitely threw it in the fucking trash the second time, he thought, drying off.

The phone by his bedside rang, interrupting Franco's thoughts. He jogged to the bedroom and lifted the phone off the receiver.

"Hello?"

"Hey, sweetie!" Sophia's said.

Her kind tone saturated his eardrums and immediately alleviated some of his distress.

"Babe! I miss you!" he squealed.

He could hear the surprise in Sophia's voice after his googly reply. It even shocked Franco and he was the one who conjured it.

While they'd only lived together for a short period of time, normally he relished in his solo weeks. They were the only times he could accumulate and admire his dark calling. She wouldn't be home for a few more days but, for the first time, he wished she'd just drop everything and come back to him.

"Wow, you're in a mood," she snickered. "I miss you too. Are you doing anything fun?"

"Just exploring some ideas for a few side projects. But I won't have any photo sessions until mid-next week. What about you?"

"*Ugh,* it's too boring to even talk about. We're basically trapped in a room for the next forty-eight hours. We just build up our pitches, only to immediately tear them down. It's the definition of insanity; the same thing over and over and expecting a different result."

The explanation resonated with him more than he expected it to. It was a familiar theme that was leeching onto him as of late.

"Sadly, I really don't have much time right now," Sophia continued. "I'm hoping to call again within the next two days, though. But don't be surprised if I can't, things have been crazy."

"No worries," Franco insisted. "I know how it can be. Besides, you know me—I've always got something to do." There was an uncommon hint of sadness in his tone. "But good luck, I love you."

"I know you do. An artist as talented as you should always be creating. I can't wait to see what you come up with next. I love you too. Bye!"

"Bye," he said, detaching himself and returning to his morning routine. But subconsciously, he also returned to his prior thoughts.

Franco started to get dressed, but for what exactly he remained unsure. He passed the bedroom door. It sat partially open. At the end of the hallway stood the dark amber door to his study.

I should see if it's the same still...

He zipped up his pants and took a few steps into the hallway. Something about the door frightened him—likely the idea of being confronted by something he had no way of controlling. Horror like no other may await.

"Fuck that, I—I need to wake up first. I need a coffee."

Franco turned his back on the study, unenthusiastic about confronting the problem first thing in the morning, and headed for the front door.

THE SUBTLE SLUMS

With a large latte in hand, Franco stepped out of the Java Hole and onto the sidewalk. The bustle of the countless people rushing around was somehow comforting to him. Normally, it was something he hated, something he yearned to escape the moment he encountered it. But this was the dawn of a new day.

They kept his mind occupied.

They helped him overlook his circumstance.

They made things feel normal.

The stress ball in his sternum was starting to break down. The silliness of the entire thing… how could he let himself believe such nonsense? *What, do you believe in ghosts now?* His lips contorted into a grin until he stepped around the building.

It was impossible! His eyes mustn't have been working right!

There was the alley.

The *exact* same alley from the re-rendered stock photo.

"No, it can't be…" Franco whispered, dread oozing off his words.

His opinion didn't matter now. The reality presented to him snuffed out what he wished he was seeing.

Flashes of light, and what he remembered on the stock photo, ripped through his brain. There sat the same scummy, olive-colored dumpster and the deteriorating cardboard box. They held the precise placement from how he'd initially viewed them. It was like he was gawking at the stock photo in real life. Everything was there.

Everything except the girl…

Franco didn't know whether to be excited or alarmed by her absence. He turned back as the hairs on his neck jumped. Looking around the crowd of people, he searched for the pretty face living rent-free in his head.

Who the fuck is she?

The faces ahead weren't anywhere near as gorgeous. Even so, as stunning as she was, it would've been difficult to pick her out of such a massive crowd. He'd only seen her face twice. Franco had given up on looking for her. Yet still, as he stepped out of the commuting chaos and into the vacant alley, he couldn't shake the feeling that someone was watching.

This doesn't feel right. What the fuck is going on?

He turned back to what felt like a manufactured scene. How could it be real? How could it just appear before is eyes? It was impossible to ignore. He couldn't just turn his back on the alley and act like it didn't exist. He had to investigate. Otherwise, the curiosity would eat him alive for as long as he lived. Franco had no idea what he was looking for if anything, but nonetheless, he approached the dumpster and peered inside.

It was bare.

Must've just been emptied.

A chill rattled his body again—the feeling of eyes on him. He whipped around, looking back to the street and the sea of people. Again, there was nothing out of the ordinary.

No one seems to be watching, so why do I feel this way?

Franco squatted, shifting his attention from the dumpster to the cardboard box. It was partially open, a darkness inside that offered him no clues.

CAME WITH THE FRAME

He sipped his drink suspiciously, glaring at the brown exterior, before setting it on the ground and inching closer. When he opened the top flaps, he found a manilla envelope inside. He scrounged around a bit longer but there was nothing else to be had. Franco ripped the envelope open. He removed a compact gridded pad, the front page of which was separated into many tiny squares. As he flipped through each sheet of paper, it became clear they were blank.

Until he reached the final page.

The single handwritten message read: "ONCE YOU'VE FOUND THE GREEN BEETLE, JUST FOLLOW THE NEEDLE."

There was some weight inside the envelope. He tilted it sideways and an antique compass slid out onto his palm. The navigation device still appeared to be functional, despite its rusted exterior and the wear of decades upon it. The tiny numbers around the star were so faded they were barely readable, but the four directions remained legible.

"The green beetle?" he whispered.

Somehow, he expected it to make sense. But none of it did. There was a sense of urgency now, stirring inside him. It was time to leave. He had no idea what the answer was but sensed it was close to home.

RESERVATIONS

"What the fuck?" Franco said. "No. Not again…"

He could barely get the words out. His eyes had to be deceiving him, yet nothing was changing. The black frame still sat on the coffee table, precisely where it had been. It even had a picture of the beach inside. The only problem was, it wasn't a picture of Sophia and Franco; it was a picture of the blonde stock photo girl.

Instead of being slumped against the disgusting wall in the alley, he'd just finished fishing through, she was lying on a towel on top of soft beach sand. The stock girl looked as sexy as ever in her skimpy bikini, a blue set with white anchors on it, and she was sucking on a glistening red lollipop. The oversized sunglasses that shrouded her eyes added an enticing element of mystery to her already absurd aura. But Franco wasn't thinking about her sexiness any longer.

The phone in the study rang. Franco looked down with hesitation in his eyes. The feeling in his gut went from bad to worse. He didn't want to answer it, but his curiosity wouldn't allow him to ignore it. After the fifth ring, he reached down and held the receiver to his ear as if the person calling was supposed to say something first.

"H—Hello?" a male voice with a French accent finally asked.

"Yes?" Franco said.

"Is this Francisco Booth?"

"Yeah…"

"Mr. Booth, good day, this is Raphael, from The Anchor. I'm just calling to confirm your eight o'clock dinner reservation. We have some guests that remain on a waiting list, but I assume you'll still be joining us, yes?"

Franco squinted at the photo of the sexy stock girl in the frame again. Suddenly, the anchor pattern on her bikini didn't seem so coincidental.

"Mr. Booth?" Raphael asked.

"Sorry…" Franco responded, trying to figure out his response. "Um, this may be a stupid question. But who booked this again?"

A moment of awkward silence wedged between the conversation.

"Why, you did, sir…" Raphael replied.

Franco's heart began to race. His eyes darted back to the photo.

"Is that okay?" the man asked. "Do you need us to cancel?"

"No…" Franco muttered. "No, everything's fine." His reply was the understatement of his lifetime.

"Okay, we'll see you soon then, Mr. Booth."

"Um, just a minute, please."

"Yes?"

"Where exactly is the restaurant located?"

"Just outside of Grace Ridge. About eleven miles off exit thirteen if you're taking the interstate."

"Grace Ridge?"

"Yes sir, is that a problem?"

Franco continued to stare at the photo, unable to make sense of it. He certainly hadn't made the reservation, but if he explained that, then there would be no means to unravel the mystery.

Franco cleared his throat. "No. Thank you."

"Alright then, sir. We look forward to giving you a *unique* experience tonight."

"Ok—"

The line went dead before Franco could finish. He looked back at the photo of the woman. As he thought about the conversation he'd just had, he grew more aggravated and slammed the phone down.

"I couldn't have set up a reservation at The Anchor. I don't even know where the fuck The Anchor is! This is madness!"

His anger grew. He didn't know why he was fuming, but there was a strange sense that he was no longer able to control his own trajectory anymore. Despite the annoyance, his curiosity was king. It controlled him.

He looked down at his watch. Just past noon.

Grace Ridge is about seven hours away, he thought. *If I leave soon, there's just enough time to make it. How can there be just enough time? It's too perfect.*

There were no easy answers to be picked out of the sky. Franco's instincts told him to just forget about it.

Get rid of the frame.

Get rid of the photo.

Get rid of the idea that something was happening.

But when he looked upon the beautiful skin of the stock photo girl and the voluptuous curves of her body, he realized that this was more than just about curiosity alone. Even to a man that made his living meandering around model types and slews of smug socialites, this woman was irresistible.

Franco lifted the frame again and studied it even more carefully this time.

Suddenly, the anger seeped out through his skin. He was calm as a cow again. He remembered his life's work. No matter how bizarre his odyssey was becoming, he still had his goals.

This is it… She's the one!

He gazed into her black shades again, licking his lips. A giant smirk crawled across his face.

You're so gorgeous that I could add you to my collection as you are, but what would be the fun in that?

THE ANCHOR

After double-checking a few maps, Franco hit the road. The erection pushing against the front of his pants took hours to subside. The excitement of meeting such a physical specimen was otherworldly.

She'll be there, in the flesh. I have so many questions, he thought.

He'd never taken exit thirteen before. Franco had driven by it on several road trips, but Grace Ridge wasn't exactly an attraction.

The long, winding roads were lined with giant rocks and dense wilderness. The occasional house popped up every few miles, but nothing remotely noteworthy.

Eventually, the pure daylight transitioned to dusk. An eerie, lighter shade of darkness encircled him as he pushed onward. Suddenly, off in the distance, he saw glowing orange light within a cluster of pines.

"That's gotta be it," Franco said. He looked at his watch; exactly five minutes remained until 8 pm. As he drew closer to the area, he saw the simple wooden sign. It was dark brown with a white, cursive font reading 'The Anchor' and included a carving of the nautical weight's outline. "No doubt about it."

Franco pulled down the rural driveway, and after a long stretch of gravel, he gazed upon the structure. The modern building and overall outward elegance made the restaurant seem out of place. As he drove closer, he noticed there was *exactly* one parking space that remained free.

Franco pulled in and exited his vehicle. Outside the building, he heard the silence that surrounded him. A sense of isolation struck his heart, making it skip a beat.

You're really doing this...

While the tension in his body screamed for him to turn back, that wasn't who he was. The thirst for answers possessed him—he had to go inside.

The interior was even more gorgeous and elegant. The décor within offered a warm charm that felt homey. The staff seemed organized and sure of themselves, all dressed up in white-top tuxedos with dark dress pants.

Classical music flowed gently in the background. The food was plated in the most attentive manner. The dishes in front of the patrons looked closer to works of art than meals—almost too beautiful to eat. Everyone inside sat with a smile on their face; how could they not at such a venue?

The maître d approached Franco, "Good evening, sir? May I take your coat?" His French accent made Franco wonder if he was the man he'd spoken with on the phone.

Franco handed him his jacket as he continued to take in the impressive establishment. Even for a guy like him, the place seemed special.

The maître d placed his jacket on a wooden rack with dozens of others near the entrance.

"Thanks," Franco replied.

"Of course, sir. May I have your name, please?" he asked, pointing his white glove at a reservation book on the counter.

"It's—um, you might have it down as Franco—or Francisco."

The maître d tapped his finger on the sheet and looked back up at his guest. A wide grin stretched across his face.

"Thank you, right this way Mr. Booth. We've saved our finest table for you."

The maître d led Franco to a candlelit table in the corner. The area was a bit distant from the rest, offering privacy and a view of the wilderness made the seat a truly prime location.

The maître d kindly pulled out a chair.

Franco nodded, stumbling over his words. "Oh, that's—that's alright, you don't have to—"

"It's quite my pleasure," he interrupted. "John-Pierre, your server, will be along momentarily."

Before the maître d left, he handed Franco a compact menu. He looked at it curiously. "Ah, one thing."

The maître d turned back.

"Should I wait to order? I mean... I'm waiting for someone, right?"

The maître d furrowed his brow. "I'm not sure, sir, are you?"

"I thought I was..."

"The register had you listed as a reservation for one. In fact, I'm not sure if you noticed, but *all* of the reservations here are for one..."

Franco took a gander around the room, shocked he hadn't noticed it before. The entire place was filled with men and women dining alone, despite an empty seat being positioned across from each person. No one seemed particularly sad about it. On the contrary, they seemed quite overjoyed by their singularity.

Feasting.

Drinking.

Tasting.

Smiling.

"Oh," Franco said. "I'm sorry. I didn't realize th—"

"It's quite alright, Mr. Booth," the maître d interrupted, breaking away from the table. "Just enjoy yourself."

While he awaited his server, Franco scanned the fancy menu, searching for something but he didn't quite understand what.

"Welcome, Mr. Booth," a waiter said approaching the table. "I'm John Pierre. It's my pleasure to serve you this evening."

Franco looked up from the menu. The server was a tightly dressed, attractive man. His clean-cut presentation reminded Franco of his own, outside of what sounded like the remnants of a French accent, which made the server more exotic.

"Happy to be here, of course," Franco replied.

While Franco was still upset in knowing that the stock girl wasn't coming, the environment at The Anchor had stolen some of his intrigue. Disappointment mulled around his mind, but he didn't want to allow it to ruin his entire evening. He'd driven quite a distance to be there and would find a way to make the best of it.

Looking back to the menu, Franco furrowed his brow. "So, um, John-Pierre, there aren't any prices on the menu…"

The server grinned. "Correct."

"How am I supposed to know—"

"There is no price because there is no price, Mr. Booth. Order whatever you desire."

"What do you mean?"

"It's been taken care of."

"Wait, what? By who?"

"On the house, sir."

"But why?"

"Here, everything here is on the house."

"That seems a bit—"

"So, do you know what you'd like to order?"

Franco took another look at the limited menu and his eyes popped. Its listing was intensely bizarre. Every dish on the sheet he'd had before. Some were more specific than others, but it was easy for him to remember because they were all *his* favorites.

How could they know? Did I tell them when I booked this reservation—

His thought was interrupted by John-Pierre. "Would you prefer a suggestion?"

Franco narrowed his eyes. It had been a long drive. He'd only stopped once to piss at a gas station and get a drink. There was a question on his mind that he felt odd asking, but cleared his throat nonetheless. "Well, actually, I was wondering, since I'm incredibly hungry, and it's already been taken care of… May I order two items off the menu?"

"Absolutely, in fact, I recommend it."

"Wonderful!"

Franco found himself lost in the mystery of The Anchor. In an odd way, it was better than he'd expected. An inexplicable feeling made him completely at home with the others he was set to dine with. Despite their namelessness and detachment, Franco was ready to enjoy his evening.

"Then I'll have the tuna tartare with avocado to start," he said, "followed by the crab-stuffed filet mignon and whiskey peppercorn sauce."

"Marvelous choice, Mr. Booth. You strike me as a rare man—is that how you'd like the steak cooked?"

"You guessed right, John-Pierre," Franco said with a wink. "I like it a little bloody."

John-Pierre grinned. "And to drink?"

"Any suggestions?"

"For you, we have a '66 Domaines Barons de Rothschild Chateau Lafite. It's twenty-five years old, almost to the day. If you're going to drink, there is no finer choice."

"66? That's the year I was born…"

John-Pierre smiled. "Well, it seems I've made a good choice then."

"Okay."

"I will return at once," John-Pierre said, stepping away.

The year felt a little too coincidental, but Franco decided to just go with it. What else was he going to do? He was starving. The weirdness would work itself out one way or another. He scanned the other guests inside the restaurant, looking for answers. There was nothing out of the ordinary.

The sudden uncorking of the bottle broke Franco's train of thought. John-Pierre poured him a generous glass. It dripped a bit more lethargically from the bottle spout than other wines that had graced his palette. John-Pierre set what remained of the bottle on the table beside the cutlery.

Franco lifted his glass and tipped it back. He let a mouthful rest on his palate before gulping it down. His eyes widened.

"Fucking delicious."

HIT THE HEAD

The meal was nothing short of exquisite. As Franco chewed on the final piece of steak on his plate, he grabbed the bottle of wine and refilled his massive glass.

Once Franco finished pouring, the wine level dipped just below the halfway mark. He set the bottle back down on the table and noticed something out of the corner of his eye. Through the transparent glass, Franco caught a glimpse at the backside of the label. A message scribbled in black read 'FRANCO, GO TO THE RESTROOM.'

"What the fuck?" Franco whispered.

John-Pierre's voice interjected. "Is everything alright, Mr. Booth? Is there something else I can get for you?"

Franco studied the Frenchman, trying to determine if he was in the know. John-Pierre had given him the bottle. A bottle that he was told was many decades old yet, somehow, coincidentally or otherwise, had a message within that was timely and targeted. Despite the sophisticated atmosphere inside The Anchor, it wasn't without its quirks. But were the unorthodox elements just part of the charm, or was it something else?

Franco looked away from the message to John-Pierre. "Ah—no, I think I'm all set."

"Well, I've certainly enjoyed serving you this evening." He nodded before leaving. "Good luck."

Franco struggled to put the puzzle together. He was looking at a message in a bottle that was as old as him, during his reservation for one—a reservation he was told he had made at an establishment he'd never heard of, hinted at in a picture frame—the contents of which continued to mysteriously evolve.

Maybe I've gone mad... he thought.

"Wait, actually," Franco reconsidered, holding his finger in the air to get the server's attention, "can you just point me in the direction of the commode?"

John-Pierre turned back to Franco, a slight curl at the corner of his lips. "Of course, sir. It's just down the hall. It's the final door. You can't miss it."

He gestured down the carpet-lined vestibule.

"Thanks," Franco replied, watching him disappear into the back of the restaurant.

Franco couldn't be sure what anyone's intentions were. He still wondered about the lovely blonde in the frame that had swept him up in the strange mystery. He not only wondered how she fit into the equation, but how the series of odd events were connected. Franco's attention turned back to the bottle then darted to the hallway.

What are you doing?

As he considered his options, an odd sensation gnawed at him—was it fright or just confusion? But there was no way he could walk out of The Anchor without seeing if the message was merely a coincidence or part of a larger, inexplicably calculated effort.

Franco rose from his seat and made his way down the hall. He walked at an almost reluctant pace—it was as if he never wanted to reach his destination. Franco's heart thumped mightily inside his chest as he reached the end of the corridor.

There's nothing in there. Just go in the fucking restroom and confirm you're not crazy.

When he entered the classy men's room, the charming symphony remained, entertaining softly in the background. He examined the urinals and bathroom stalls.

Empty.

Franco furrowed his brow, trying to figure out if he was relieved or disappointed. Part of him enjoyed the weirdness while another part dreaded it.

"There's nothing here," he grumbled, torn by the revelation.

The colorful taste in his mouth that still lingered from his meal and the enchanting bathroom tunes weren't enough of a distraction to stop him from wondering. He couldn't fathom what relevance, if any, the events of the past few days had. But at least reality seemed somewhat stable again. The ordinary space provided him with some solace.

Franco sighed and approached the sink. He turned on the faucet and splashed his face with water.

Why did I even come here? Because of a picture? There's nothing here. It's time to go.

The lights in the bathroom violently flickered.

The soothing music in the background cut out when the electrical hiccups started, and after several flashes, there was no longer just a black and white checkered wall depicted behind him in the mirror. There was a face. But it wasn't *just* a face, it was an impossible sight. The mangled head of Cassie, the call girl, hovered directly behind him.

The blood gushing from the exposed meat and the flaps of flesh on her cheeks rained down on Franco's shoulder. Her ruined jaw was slack and the glowing beams in her eye sockets reflected in the mirror.

The shock zapped him, causing his jaw to chatter as he noticed her leaky head wasn't attached to anything. The remnants of the girl levitating over him started to tremor. Blood continued to pour from the gaping wound as Cassie's zombified voice echoed off the tiled walls.

"I still glow for you," she groaned.

Franco screamed and ran for the door.

As he bolted out into the hallway, the lights continued to flicker. Upon reaching the dining area, Franco noticed many of the other patrons seemed equally disturbed. But what really drew his attention was the once neglected chairs at each of their tables, which were now occupied. Each seat was filled with a different blood-drenched or mutilated individual.

A man with a pulverized head and no arms shook violently in his seat. The juicy pile of extra-rare roast beef that had once been his face flapped about offering no undiscernible expression.

A woman with her head hanging and neck snapped sideways, the splintered bone pressed against her blue skin like an excited erection trying to escape pants. A small boy standing on his chair, naked and castrated with a filleted penis—his sexual organs torn to shreds before he could even figure out what their purpose was.

Each of the atrocities were all unique, but also had one thing in common. The individuals sitting across from the ravaged bodies all had the same look in their eyes; familiarity. It was the same look that Franco had when looking at Cassie's ghoulish face in the men's room. It seemed he wasn't the only one with demons in the dining room.

Screams erupted throughout the dining room. Many of the other victims were ripped to ribbons, their vital organs exposed or extracted. Just as Franco had seen with Cassie in the restroom, the mutilations surrounding him were so gruesome that the bodies surrounding him couldn't have been alive. Even outside of the ghastly injuries, the victims were beyond repair and overcome with rot, insects, and oozing decomposition fluids.

Still, there they remained, animated as ever.

Franco could still feel the warm caress of Cassie's blood all over his suit. He looked back to the table he'd just been seated at—another impossible sight.

Cassie's head had somehow found the plate that he'd just finished eating his steak out of. One of the eerie flashlight 'eyes' jammed into her disfigured head activated and then deactivated.

She was winking at him

Crying out again, Franco ran for the door. Many of the patrons did the same, but when a woman reached for the front door's handle, only a clicking sound was heard.

"It's locked!" she shrieked.

As the crowd bottle-necked near the exit, Franco felt someone tap his shoulder.

"I hope you enjoyed your meal!" the maître d screamed. "Don't forget your coat, Mr. Booth!"

The employee looked far different from the charming gentleman he'd exchanged words with upon entry. His eyes glowed red with rage, his face rotten down to the bone. As he pushed the jacket into Franco's chest, the maître d's forearm snapped sideways. A blood-curdling screech erupted from his congested and maggoty airways.

Fright fueling his actions, Franco turned away from the disturbing maître d and bumped into another man. He was a bit older than Franco, but every bit as horrified by what was unfolding.

"They're back!" the man cried. "How the fuck are they back?! I cut his little cock off." Tears dripped down his cheeks as he pulled at his thinning hair. "He's dead! He's *fucking dead!*"

John-Pierre dragged himself toward the men. "You might've forgotten about them," he whispered, "but they haven't forgotten about you."

The server's flesh was not how Franco recalled just minutes ago. It had transformed. A putrid, necrotic slime lubricated his now bloated exterior. The fingernails at his sides looked as sharp as daggers. His teeth were as yellow as butter, and his grin was wide enough for the world. The cold stare that projected from his inflamed eyes was enough to strike fear into the fearless.

Franco's normally olive complexion went white. A grave sensation came over him. He started to backpedal and pushed the child killer away. The pedophile fell into John-Pierre's demonic clutches within the logjam at The Anchor's entrance doors.

The waiter's sharp, yellow teeth sunk deep into the throat of the child killer. Like a rabid dog, John-Pierre bit down and tore side to side, tugging at the skin and meat underneath until the inside of the man's throat was exposed. A generous gush of blood sprayed like a busted pipe, spattering the horrified guests.

"Why's everyone so fucking scared?!" John-Pierre asked. "Shouldn't be that unfamiliar!"

With the exit route locked, Franco decided to make his own. He slipped on his jacket and lifted one of the chairs from a vacated table. As he smashed it into the window, the glass broke much easier than he could've imagined. The shower of shards crashed down, multiplying the sharp fragments over and over.

Franco jumped out the window and onto the crystalized mulch in front of the building. Running back to the parking lot, he kept his eyes on his car.

Almost there!

He shoved his hand into his pocket and rummaged around inside his jacket, searching for his keys. Franco pulled one out, but it wasn't the set he was expecting. It was a lone silver ring that held a single golden skeleton key.

"What the—where the hell did this come from?" he asked himself.

Screams and the sound of glass breaking distracted Franco from the key. The shards around the edges of the window in front of The Anchor broke away as the bloody patrons and pulverized bodies poured out of the building. Through the opening, Franco saw Cassie's glowing eyes hovering in the background. The levitating head continued to bleed over the crowd as it exited the building.

"Fuck! Fuck! Fuck!" Franco screeched.

CAME WITH THE FRAME

He tucked away the mysterious key and dug through his pockets again. Relief washed over him when he felt the familiar cluster of metal.

"Got 'em!" he said, removing the keys from the pocket.

Unlocking the door, Franco hopped inside and started the car. As terrified as he was, his compulsion still throbbed inside him. His brain screamed to stomp on the gas, but his heart told him to wait.

The glistening guts and screams of horror were typically music to his ears. From the safety of his car, he watched the hellish mutilations in pursuit, captivated by their beauty. Seeing his art beside so many other private collections was breathtaking.

After a moment of indulgence, his survival instincts kicked in again. He raced away, kicking up gravel. As Franco fled the madness of the restaurant, a cloud of dirt rose behind the car before anyone could catch up with him.

DIAL OUT

The bedroom mirror didn't help convince him he wasn't going mad. Not only had he seen the bloodstains that Cassie's phantom head had left all over him, but he'd also *felt* the warmth from the gore he'd been drenched in. It was a distinct feeling—something that he was certain of.

But now he stood in front of his dresser after a seven-hour car ride without a splotch of blood on him. It was the latest rung on a ladder of mysteries. At the rate he was going, the ladder might take him into the clouds. The discomfort and uncertainty swelling in his mind had finally reached a fever pitch.

He looked at his reflection. "Welp, I'm fucking crazy. I am. I guess that's it! Not many other options!" Franco laughed manically as he took a more intimate look at his face in the mirror. He pointed at his reflection and aggressively argued with it. "You've been turning girls inside out for years, making them into art—and just *now*, all of a sudden, *you're* crazy?! Ridiculous! You've *been* crazy, and you'll stay crazy! Everything's fine."

Franco erupted into a fit of hysteria. Falling onto the carpet, he clutched at his gut, his belly aching from the intense laughing fit.

The sleep deprivation also wasn't helping him any. Franco hadn't pulled an all-nighter in a long time. The inflamed blood vessels in his eyeballs offered a telltale sign. There wasn't a hell of a lot keeping him balanced the last few days. Sophia still hadn't called him. While he could've used her calming presence more than ever, it was probably for the best that she didn't see him in such a state. As he continued to roll around in stitches, another idea hit him.

"The frame!" he squealed. "Of course! It's time to check on it! It never stops! What surprise is gonna be waiting inside it for me this time?!"

Franco rushed out of his bedroom. He chuckled his way down the hall and burst into his study. The wicked, black frame sat waiting for him on the coffee table just as expected. The stock photo inside was once again different than before.

"What now?!" Franco yelled, picking it up.

This time, the seductive stock girl was leaning back against the wall of a deteriorating phone booth. Judging from the various scribble that defaced the communication cell it must've been located in a rough part of the city. The beautiful girl wore a leather jacket with a ripped tee shirt underneath. Her sandy blonde hair now had a darker, wetter look. A cigarette was pressed to her cherry lips, held between her matching nails.

Out of the blue, all the laughs that Franco had been drumming up died out. The sudden seriousness infected him. "It's… it's just not possible," Franco whispered.

He looked closer at the obscene language graffitied on the phone booth. One scribble stood out from the rest.

'FOR A GOOD TIME CALL 401-555-5555.'

I shouldn't, Franco thought. *Why would I? None of this feels right. Nothing good can come of it.*

He looked at the number again, then at the telephone. The morbid maverick inside him couldn't resist—he had to know.

"I've come this far," he said, reaching for the phone.

He punched in the numbers but heard no ringing. A strange, crackling noise bubbled on the other end of the line. Then, a voice bled through. Franco struggled to hear it.

"Franco?" a woman asked.

"Who is this?" Franco demanded.

"Did you enjoy your dinner?"

"How—How are you getting inside my house?"

"You're a generational talent—"

The connection started to fade in and out, and he missed some of what she was saying.

"Hello? Hello?!" Franco cried.

The scrambled voice swelled until it finally patched back in. "And I know about your collection. Your skeletons are beautiful. So beautiful that I've decided I'd like to become one of them. If you don't afford me that courtesy, then I'll have no choice but to expose you and your entire box of secrets. But to—"

"Wait, what—"

"Silence!" she demanded. "I haven't much time to relay this message! Before I can be added to your marvelous collection, you'll first have to locate me. Which is why I gave you the compass. So, make sure you have it handy because *today's* the day. Rest assured, the green beetle isn't far."

"Are you the woman from the photo?!" Franco yelled.

"I have to go now," she said, her voice crackling until it was unintelligible.

"Wait!" Franco begged.

The phone line went dead.

Franco looked at his bookcase that acted as the barrier between the world and his darkest secrets. Dumbfounded by the revelations on the phone call, he wondered how the woman knew of his horrors. An inner urge told him to check on his sanctuary of perversion.

Grabbing the candle stick, Franco reached into his pocket. Unintentionally he produced the gold skeleton key that he found in his jacket while escaping The Anchor. He had no idea what it was for but decided it best to keep it.

He fished in his jacket once again, this time retrieving the small silver key that led to his hidden art. As the bookshelf slid sideways, Franco's heart thumped wildly in his chest.

The red lights lit up the room and revealed another hook set waiting on the wall. The lonely frame hanger stared back at him. Under normal circumstances, it wouldn't have been something that he thought twice about, but Franco hadn't placed it there himself. What the girl on the phone claimed was true—he was no longer the only person who had been afforded a glimpse at the many skeletons in his closet.

GREEN BEETLE

Franco stood in his driveway, entranced in deep thought. The estate had a spacious, beautiful front yard surrounded by privacy bushes. With his camera bag slung over his shoulder, he exhaled deeply. He didn't know exactly when he would need the camera, but he wanted to be ready.

Imagine that, he thought. *Turning a stock photo into a work of art. That could be my greatest accomplishment yet. That's what she's asking for. I suppose if anyone can do it, it's me.*

The idea of capturing her was alluring. He'd never had a fan of his 'honest' work before. She was so entranced by it that she wanted to become an extension of it. Or did she?

He would've been an idiot to not wonder if there was an ulterior motive at stake. But why even play with fire? She knew he was a killer, and also knew exactly where the irrefutable evidence of his crimes hung, and yet, she hadn't called the police.

Twisted cunt wants me to carve her up. That I can do. I have to now, really. Nothing more that I hate more than loose ends.

Regardless of her reasoning, he would have to treat the situation like he would any other photo session; shoot first and sort through the images afterward. And he needed to find her sooner than later.

As he wandered through his yard, carefully examining the various plant life, Franco reached into his jacket and pulled out the compass for the fourth time. There was no reaction on his face, but his expression was tired—he was exhausted.

How long am I gonna do this? Butterflies, grasshoppers, a few ants. That's all that's out here. I've never seen a fucking green beetle around here… not once. His eyes grew heavier, but he couldn't sleep while his life was hanging in the balance. *I need to get the hell out of here for a bit. Maybe some food will help.*

Franco turned away from the shrub and opened the door of his car. He plopped his unwashed body down into the driver's seat of his car and turned over the engine.

"You'll figure it out," he mumbled. He set the camera bag on the passenger seat and looked at the antique compass in his hand. "Stupid thing." He unzipped the main crease on his bag and slipped it inside.

As Franco left his driveway, he noticed a car parked across the road, directly in front of the property. The vehicle stood out because, in Franco's posh neighborhood, cars were rarely parked on the street. Though stopped, the car was still running. The most unsettling aspect was that all the vehicle's windows were completely blacked out.

It took him a moment to comprehend what he was seeing, but eventually, it clicked. The olive-colored paint job and the signature compact frame of the famous Volkswagen model stared back at him.

"Green fucking beetle!" he yelled.

The beetle accelerated down the street.

Franco took off and tailed it, keeping pace as best he could, but the car was driving erratically, blowing through stop signs and traffic lights regardless of the color. But Franco wasn't about to let the car escape. The mystery was suddenly within grasp.

He wanted what he'd been promised on the phone and needed his skeletons to remain closeted. But more than anything, he needed to know what the fuck was going on.

Franco followed the green beetle onto the highway. But the section they'd gotten into only had a couple of exits to go before they reset. That stretch of highway ended at Exit 65 and then restarted again with Exit 1. But as they approached it, Franco noticed somehow, there was one more exit ramp ahead.

"What the fuck?" he said.

A new sign appeared.

EXIT 66.

Despite it being the middle of the day, their surroundings grew darker. Franco looked at his watch. When his eyes came back to the road, an ominous black void invaded the freeway ahead. Franco rubbed his tired eyes and looked into the blackness, utterly perplexed.

"It's not even noon yet?!"

Something slammed against the rear window of the green Beetle, causing it to spiderweb. Seconds later, the tinted glass was blown out completely. A flood of fragments erupted everywhere, scraping down the highway asphalt. Franco swerved wildly to avoid most of the pieces. He focused on the Beetle's missing rear window, staring into its void. Franco squinted. Then his eyes widened with shock and horror.

My first… Franco suddenly recalled. *Ashley drove a green Beetle…*

A ghastly face appeared in the blown-out window, striking profound fear into Franco's heart. Ashley's hollowed-out forehead oozed a fresh gush of crimson. Despite the bulky, telephoto lens having been forced into the space where the critical areas of her brain resided, she still managed to smirk.

"No!" Franco screamed. "You're dead! You're all supposed to be dead!"

As Ashley brandished her teeth, blood drizzled through the cracks, her white eyes locking on Franco. Her rotten hands adjusted the lens wedged in her skull as if sizing Franco up for a photo shoot.

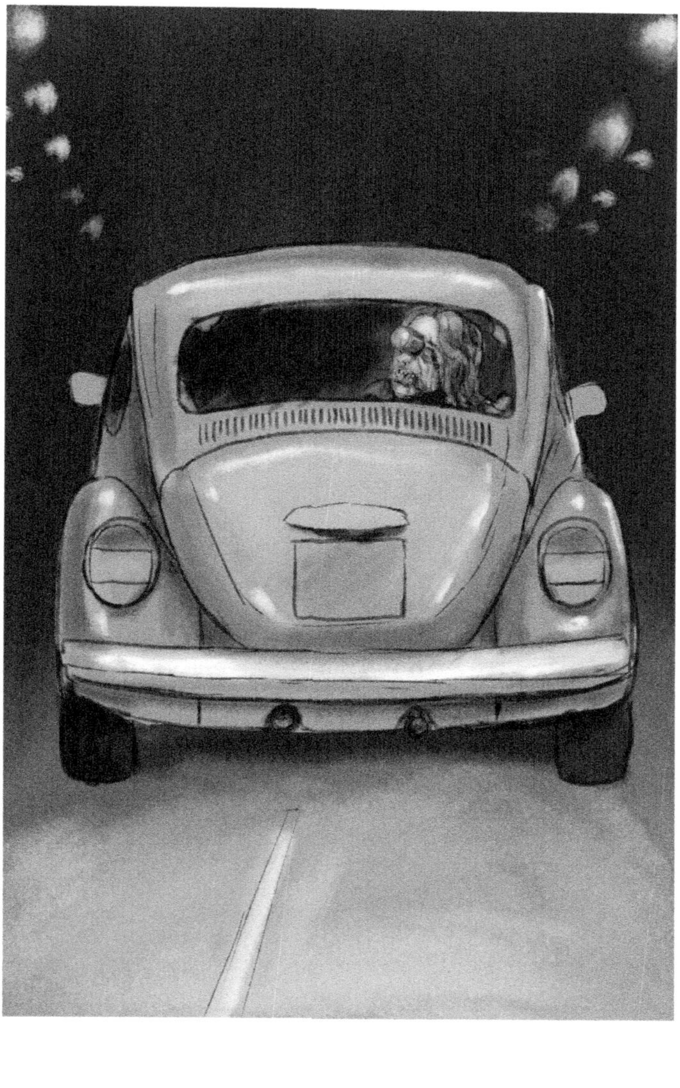

A massive flash, many times the power of the standard camera, flooded out the back of the vehicle. The pitch-black atmosphere of the exit that didn't exist slowly transitioned until it was eliminated by the white-out of flashes.

Franco no longer had a path to follow in front of him. Panic set in as he stared into the extraordinary flash, his eyes pulsating with agony as he lost control of the steering wheel. His equilibrium turned upside down and he was tossed around the car as it tumbled. While his body rag-dolled side to side, Franco belted out a scream, blinded by the whiteness.

THE FINAL PIECE

The car lay upside down and totaled, but somehow Franco got through the ordeal unscathed.

Seatbelts really do work, I guess, he thought.

Franco sat suspended upside down, held firmly in place by the safety strap. He glanced out the window and saw a wooded area encircled by trees. He looked from side to side—Ashley and the green Beetle were nowhere to be seen. It was still dark outside, so all the finer details of Franco's surroundings remained unknown. He pressed the release button on the seatbelt, but it failed to set him free.

"Damn," he mumbled.

His camera bag was on the roof of the car, which, due to the vehicle's current positioning, was within arm's length. Franco unzipped the sack and sifted through the contents before extracting his tripod. He carefully unscrewed the makeshift leg cover, revealing the same spikey tip he'd shoved through Cassie's face. He stabbed at the seatbelt with the razor siding and tip of the device, and after several attempts, Franco was able to cut himself free. Upon release, he fell onto the ceiling and gathered his bearings. Franco located the busted-out driver's side window and slipped out of the vehicle.

He looked into the darkness, still unsure what the answer was. Seeing dead girls that were somehow still functional had become the norm. He had no idea what came next, but he didn't feel like standing around.

Franco hunched defensively, keeping the tripod spear steady in hand as he slung the camera bag over his shoulder. The sound of metal thudding against sand found his ears. He looked down at his feet.

The compass!

Franco scooped the corroded navigational tool out of the dirt, then zipped up his camera bag, grateful that the happy accident had given him something. Franco tapped against the face of the device and squinted, trying to see through the fogged glass.

The needle shot out to the right, pointing toward a batch of thick trees that harbored a faint amber glow. He was tired—exhausted by the whole ordeal. The anger in his chest made him happy to hold his terminal tripod. He caressed the tip thirsting for blood.

Feeling heat on his palm, it was clear the compass was doing something. The needle inside glowed red and pointed into the darkness. Franco didn't hesitate. He took off, jogging in the direction the crimson needle pointed. After several minutes, he saw the faint glow of a lantern in the distance.

The flicker of flame sat hanging on a tree limb that had been jammed into the ground. As Franco drew closer, he saw a small staircase comprised of dirt and dead leaves leading to a black door buried underground. Aside from being metal, the door looked no different from any door he'd ever seen at the entrance of a home. But its location was curious, to say the least.

The subterranean path didn't frighten him, he was riddled with excitement. Anxious to resolve the mystery that had tormented him for days. He looked at the strange compass, the weathered needle aligned directly with the bunker door. Franco smiled, a flicker of madness in his eyes.

"It's time," he whispered.

Clenching the tripod spike, Franco descended the steps in a methodical fashion. As he approached the bottom, he slipped the compass into his pocket and noticed a sentence in red lettering on the door that read: ONLY YOU CAN OPEN ME.

He tried the doorknob, but to his surprise, it was locked. Franco's eyes sparked and a smile crept up on his face. *It's all coming together,* he thought, feeling around in his jacket. He retrieved the golden skeleton key. The one he'd found in his pocket after recovering his jacket from the murderous maître d at The Anchor.

"This has to be it," he whispered, inserting the metal teeth into the lock.

It didn't turn.

Franco furrowed his brow, a look of befuddlement overcoming him. "What the hell?" He reread the words on the door again. "*Only you can open me.* It doesn't make sense." Suddenly, it struck him. "It never makes sense!"

Franco rushed back up the stairs. In the distance, he could still see the outline of his crumpled vehicle. Franco ran to the car and slipped back inside through the broken window. He reached for the steering wheel and yanked the keys out of the ignition.

When he returned to the black door in the woods, he was out of breath. But based on what the door asked of him, he guessed it could only be one key.

A key that only he knew the use for.

A key that kept his skeletons veiled.

The key to his darkness.

The silver key's jagged teeth slipped into the lock perfectly. When the rusty door creaked open, only darkness lay ahead. Franco entered eagerly, anxious to bring his morbid odyssey to a close and ready to create his greatest masterpiece.

"Hello?" Franco asked.

No one answered.

The light that crept inside from the door allowed Franco to see a thin string that hung from a lightbulb in the center of the room. As he reached for the twine to give it a tug, the door slammed shut behind him.

"Hey!" he yelled, whipping around.

Franco ran back to the door and tried to pull it open, but there was zero give. He didn't hear the door lock, but it was. Confined to the total blackout, Franco frantically searched the darkness for the string again. After taking a few steps, he felt the coarse material on his fingers again.

Regardless of his fright, when the light in the room came on, Franco hoped to see the stock girl from the photo. He still yearned to mold her into a signature piece. But the universe wasn't prepared to answer a maniac's prayers.

A small wooden chest with an oversized lock now sat on the floor. There was only one key left that seemed logical. But the way things had been playing out, he wasn't sure of anything.

Franco squatted down, stuck the golden skeleton key into the hole, and twisted. The lock popped open and he set it on the floor beside him. Carefully, Franco lifted the lid of the chest, but just as he was about to open it, the lid flung backward.

Jumping to his feet, Franco stepped back, watching the sphere appear several feet in front of him. The ball of energy, with a hellish hue, levitated near the ceiling of the room. The planet-like orb swirled above his head, doubling in speed with each revolution. Crackles of energy erupted off the sphere and scrambled down toward the new horrors it shed its crimson light upon.

What he found instead of the stock photo girl were the final, fatal expressions of his many past projects. His most perverse daydreams had become his worst nightmares. Franco looked back at the door and found himself surrounded.

"No!" he wailed. "It—it's not possible!"

His skeletons howled ages anguish with each breath.

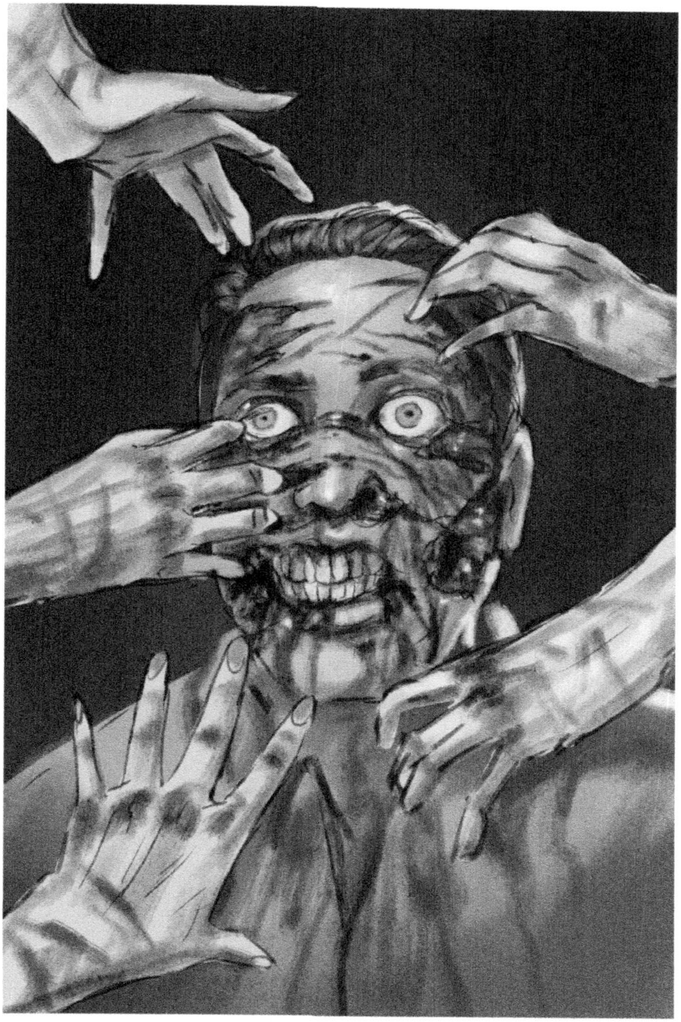

Evoked by the infernal energy of the spiraling orb above, each of the many women he'd lured to his midnight photo sessions manifested. In person, their mangled, malformed depictions were even more ghastly than the versions that hung on his walls.

The rotten faces.

The knocked-out teeth.

The gore and bones.

The maggots and worms.

It was all slowly creeping out of obscurity in the red room—gradually closing in on Franco. The monsters he loved and created. Every piece of his morbid art was represented, but in an awful way, he had never imagined possible.

His renditions of death had been given life.

The rage in their eyes festered—the fury of an accumulation of horror, seasoned to a putrid perfection. They had been ready for that moment for some time.

Franco's vocal cords shredded as he let out a blood-curdling shriek as the gore-smeared hands of the mangled women came at him from every direction. As they ripped into his body and tore him apart, a final flash, independent from the sources inside the space, illuminated the entire room.

NOT JUST BROWSING

Mia Simms pulled up to the gloomy storefront, letting out a sigh of relief. It was raining buckets outside and she needed a break from the road. With her path being absent of streetlights due to the route's sparse traffic patterns, it was becoming more difficult to see out the windshield. She was caught in the middle of the kind of storm that dropped water faster than the wipers could push it off. But despite Mother Nature's inopportune upheaval, the drive still reminded Mia of all the things she loved most about road trips.

The frequent, random pit stops.

The peculiar places she'd probably never see again.

The genuine sense of adventure that was somehow lost in life the older she grew.

The catalog of back-thought and stark self-reflection that came with a stretch of extended isolation had always been something she'd yearned for from time to time. However, Mia wished this trip hadn't been the result of such grim circumstances.

She looked at the collection of occult items lining the hazy windows.

"No way," she mumbled. "Fuck yeah, I love oddities!"

She looked at the collection of occult-ish items lining the hazy windows, then over to the black wooden signage. Squinting her eyes, she tried to see past the relentless rainfall to read the sign. "Morbid Curiosities. What a name."

Her excitement couldn't be contained. A childish grin found her face, helping her forget why she'd hit the road in the first place. It was exactly what she needed—a positive distraction not only from her life but the perils that awaited her on the lonely highway.

Mia exited the vehicle and stepped into the stormy obscurity outside her car. As she scrambled out of the fierce conditions and sprinted into the shop, a cluster of bells jingled on the entrance door.

No one was manning the register.

Mia didn't let that stop her from diving in and examining the strange relics that littered the cozy but creepy dwelling. The place had everything.

There were glass jars that contained various herbs, minerals, powders, and liquids. Shellacked animal skulls sat beside books on witchcraft and the occult. Wooden crates filled with preserved and laminated newspaper clippings boasting bizarre headlines about murders, strange creatures, and unexplained events. Used tarot cards, damaged dolls, and old Halloween costumes had a home here as well.

"Jackpot," Mia mumbled.

As Mia smelled the witchy aroma of the burning incense, she felt the place was like one giant estate sale for a collector of all things macabre. Death was in the air and she loved it.

Mia dallied down the aisles, slowing next to the items that captured her attention. She grinned. She took great pleasure in examining the strange stock, but as Mia eventually made her way to the far corner of the shop, something stuck out. As weird as the junk inside the store was, what her eye fell upon was weirder.

Along the aged wooden planks that comprised the wall hung a group of a dozen or so pictures. They were all different and yet, somehow, all the same.

Most of the dark, artistic depictions seemed to contain people deep in the clutches of dread. They were all encompassed by violence. The fierce flare of regret encapsulated in their eyes was intertwined with profound agony. They looked imprisoned—suffocated by the surrounding madness.

Once Mia's gaze found the first picture, she couldn't rip herself away from it. The imagery was terrifying. The man depicted was ensnared in the center of a cyclone of horror—a group of sadistically disfigured women had found their way into his flesh. They dug under his skin and meat, uncovering his bones, their sharp, broken nails tearing his casing as if it were tissue paper. The agony on the man's face looked otherworldly—like it had already reverberated in the afterlife a million times over.

It looked *infinite*.

A foul feeling crept up inside Mia. It wasn't even the violence portrayed in the photo that bothered her—she enjoyed macabre imagery to an extent—but there was something about the print trapped inside the creepy, ebony frame, something different than any photo she'd ever seen.

"That one's not for sale," a female voice from across the room said.

Mia shuddered and let out a small yelp, turning in the direction of the voice. "Shit—oh—hi! I—I didn't see you there."

"Sorry dear," the shopkeeper said, "I didn't intend to startle you."

Behind the counter near the backdoor stood an aged but attractive woman with a red bandana covering her head. Blonde locks crept out from the sides. The scarf, as well as the red shawl that was wrapped around her body, were both embroidered with various astrological symbols. The golden stars and pale moons were plentiful. Her lips and fingers were painted a deep purple. Calm as can be, a pair of cold, blue eyes stared at Mia. And beside each of her cheeks hung a big hoop earring.

Mia smiled kindly. "No worries, I kind of scare easy sometimes."

"Well, if you scare easily, maybe this isn't the place for you?" the woman chuckled.

"Ha, just because I scare doesn't mean that I don't like it," Mia replied. "But that's too bad about the picture. It just kinda sucks you in. It's... dark."

The shopkeeper approached her and looked at the disturbing photograph. Her icy eyes bounced away from the frame and fixed back on Mia.

"Interesting choice of words," the shopkeeper said.

Mia wasn't sure how to respond. "This is quite the place you have... I'm Mia, by the way."

She extended her hand toward the woman. Surprised by the shopkeeper, Mia wasn't sure why she felt the need to introduce herself. But the friendlier she acted, the longer she'd feel comfortable hanging around the shop and staying out of the monsoon-like conditions.

The shopkeeper accepted her gesture, and when their skin connected, a shiver that Mia did a marvelous job of masking ran down her spine.

"Venus," the shopkeeper replied.

"Like the planet?" Mia asked.

Venus nodded.

"That's so awesome."

The shopkeeper ignored her statement and pulled her hand away from Mia's. She pointed to the pictured man buried within the amalgamation of cut-up women.

"Do you know who this photo is a depiction of?" Venus asked.

Mia liked Venus' accent but was unable to place it. The foreign tongue gave her a unique feel. "No, I'm afraid not," Mia replied.

Venus' eyes darkened before looking back to the photo. "It's Francisco Booth."

Mia nodded but didn't give off the vibe that she recognized the name.

"Are you familiar with him?" Venus asked.

"Sounds familiar, but I'm not sure," Mia said.

"He was a relatively well-known photographer slash serial killer."

"Yikes."

"*Yikes* is right."

Thunder rumbled in the distance, adding to the eeriness of the story.

Venus looked back to the windows robotically, waiting for the noise to cease before continuing. "He's responsible for the slaughter of fourteen women between nineteen-seventy-two and nineteen-ninety. Booth aspired to turn women into a warped version of what he saw as 'honest' art. He took their pictures, and their lives, in terrible ways." She looked at Mia. "Unimaginable ways."

"What did he do to them?" Mia asked. She couldn't help but be curious.

"He molded them into perverse extensions of his photography equipment, combining their bodies with cameras, film, and other accessories."

"That's so bizarre."

"Disgusting is what it is."

An awkward silence separated their dialogue before Mia attempted to move it forward again.

"Is this... is this photo real?" Mia moused.

Venus clenched her jaw. "The photo's authenticity is irrelevant. What happened was most certainly real. That is all that truly matters."

Mia pointed at one of the brutalized women. "So Booth put that lens in her forehead?"

"Precisely."

"Jesus, what a psycho."

"That's not even the scariest part."

"Really?"

"It's the unanswered questions that tend to upset people the most."

"Like what?"

"Well, officially, no one actually knows what happened to him. He just kind of disappeared one day. After he went missing the police eventually searched his estate, but instead of finding him, they found a bookshelf that had been left open. A secret passage to a secret room."

Mia's eyes widened. "What was in the secret room?"

"Terrible things."

Mia remained silent and nodded, awaiting further details.

"His private collection," Venus continued. "Ghoulish framed portraits he kept of his victims—after he had his way with them."

Mia cringed when she looked at the woman in the still with the massive telephoto lens sticking out of her forehead, thinking about what the real stuff must've looked like.

"But, for all intents and purposes," Venus said, "Francisco Booth simply vanished into thin air."

"I doubt that," Mia scoffed, "he's gotta be somewhere. Which is even creepier when you think about it…"

"What? You don't believe in magic?" Venus asked brandishing a rotten smile for the first time. "That's funny."

The tarnished teeth made Mia a bit more uneasy, but she pressed on. "Why do you say that?"

"It's just, you seem so at home in a place like this, yet you don't believe."

"Don't get me wrong, I love the idea. Strange things are the most intriguing, but usually, some kind of deflating explanation eventually surfaces."

"Maybe you've come to the right place after all," Venus said, her black grin widening.

"It feels that way. When I saw your place, there was no way I was gonna just drive by it."

Mia looked back at Franco's horrified expression in the frame. It was mesmerizing.

"How do you know so much about him? I consider myself pretty well-versed in the realm of weird and creepy shit and I've never heard of him before."

"It's not surprising."

"Why do you say that?"

"The majority of serial killers only get famous if their identity is revealed while they're still alive. More than anything, people want to know the ending."

"What about Jack the Ripper or—or The Zodiac?" Mia asked.

"You may have a Jack the Ripper once a century—a case of an unknown assailant that completely captivates the public—but those are anomalies. For every one that makes the headlines another twenty fall between the cracks, never to be spoken of again. Sometimes the police won't even make it public. But all the ones on my wall, we knew who they were, but no one can say what happened to them. And because their stories are incomplete, they're often overlooked. That's what makes them so special."

The hair on Mia's neck stood up. "Well, I'm sure they're all nice and far away."

Mia looked down at a box of dusty, old frames on the floor. All the frames were unique antiques that were attractive to the eye. Still, despite all of them being vastly different styles manufactured by different companies, they all contained the exact same stock photo. The beautiful woman with unforgettable curves in the countless frames sat in a lonely blank room. A dark space where a single lightbulb hung from the ceiling and a planet-like sphere loomed in the distant darkness behind her.

The woman looked like Venus.

"Is—Is that you?" Mia asked, pointing down at the box of frames. "Are you a model or something?"

"Not exactly but in a way," Venus said.

"What do you mean?" Mia furrowed her brow. "It's either you or it isn't."

"It's a much younger me," she confessed. "These are just old things of mine, they're not for sale nor worth anything."

"That's so cool. I always wondered if the stock photo people were even real. These frames are so cool. I'd take one in a heartbeat—"

"*Again,* they're not for you!" Venus yelled.

The shift in tone took Mia by surprise. "Oh, okay…"

"I am sorry, your aura is too pure for something of this nature." Venus calmed herself. "I know these have caught your eye, my dear, but my store is quite vast. Maybe we can find something else that calls to you?" The woman smiled kindly, changing the subject. "I'll tell you what. If you have a few minutes, I have some things I can show you which have far stranger origins than some old picture frames. How does that sound?"

Mia looked out the windows. The rain was coming down even harder than when she'd entered. The road was dark and wicked. Not just in regards to the physical drive ahead, but also, the mental trials that she knew lay ahead.

The same uneasiness she'd had since she decided to turn the key in the ignition continued grinding in her gut. Alarming angst raged at just the thought of getting back inside her car again. With the already worrying motive for her sudden road trip still lingering, Mia welcomed an elongated distraction.

While initially put off by how harsh the shopkeeper was, Mia wasn't going to get back on the road anytime soon. She relaxed and allowed the initial discomfort to dissipate. The shopkeeper's temper had died down. Mia's intrigue hadn't. Surely whatever the woman planned on showing her was a better choice than sitting inside her car alone during a violent storm.

"Actually, that sounds like fun," Mia said, pulling her eyes away from the messy storm that festered outside.

Venus gave her a mischievous smile. "Wonderful."

The shopkeeper ventured back behind the counter. She stepped into the doorway behind it and held open the curtain that obscured the opening at the rear of the store. "Because I can tell that you're not just browsing—that you, in fact, have a strange passion inside you just as I have inside me—I'm prepared to show you some items from my *private* collection."

"Really?!" Mia squealed. "You have a whole separate collection from these?"

Venus nodded.

"Why do you keep it separate?"

"Because these items are beyond rare. They are *all* one-of-a-kind. And some of them are... dangerous."

Mia's eyes lit up like she'd just hit it big on a scratch ticket. "That would be amazing!"

Suddenly, an ear-ripping crack of thunder let loose outside. It sounded like a circuit breaker had exploded. The noise was so bold and invasive that it made Mia jump.

"Holy fuck!" she shrieked, as a bolt of lightning flashed in the distance.

The lights in the room cut out, and darkness enveloped every nook.

"Oh, Jesus," Mia cried.

"Stay calm," Venus said. "Sometimes when the storms get bad, the fuses fry."

An orange glow came to life on the counter as Venus ignited the oil lantern that sat behind the checkout desk. Lamp in hand, she returned to the curtain and pulled it open.

"The breaker is in the cellar," Venus said. "You may as well just come down with me."

Another soul-jarring roar of thunder erupted that was so loud that it made the entire building vibrate.

Mia didn't shriek this time, but her body shuddered like someone had just stepped on her future grave.

She looked at the woman's dimly illuminated grin. Mia didn't know exactly why she was happy, but the smirk seemed out of place. She'd watched Venus closely during the thunderous crack just moments ago—she didn't move a muscle. It was as if nothing frightened her. What had she seen to build such boldness?

Mia tried to put aside the disruption of the storm and refocus on the conversation. "Why—Why should I go down into the cellar with you?"

Venus's rotten grin stretched wider. "Because, that's where the rest of my collection is."

MIA'S MACABRE JOURNEY HAS JUST BEGUN!
TO LEARN WHAT HAPPENS NEXT, READ
MORBID CURIOSITIES BOOKS 2 & 3!

ARON BEAUREGARD'S
MORBID CURIOSITIES

BOOK 2:
THE ILLUSION OF CHOICE

ARON BEAUREGARD'S
MORBID CURIOSITIES

BOOK 3:
CEMETERY CAMP

FOR SIGNED BOOKS, MERCH, AND
EXCLUSIVE ITEMS VISIT

ABHORROR.COM

ACKNOWLEDGMENTS

Huge thanks to Kristopher Triana for helping me edit this book. Great guy—very hairy toes. Also, many thanks to the people who constantly read and promote my work on social media and elsewhere. There are too many of you to name individually, but I want each of you to know I truly appreciate you. Thanks to Daniel J. Volpe for being a good friend. Smells like a diaper full of boiled ham, but keeps it real. Huge thanks to all the other awesome people in the horror community. I look forward to seeing our strange genre continue to rise while maintaining the foul and fearless imagination that got us here.

ABOUT THE AUTHOR

Aron Beauregard doesn't exist anymore. This is the last known photo of him, oddly enough, with just one hard nipple. The Splatterpunk Award-Winning author was canceled, for a second, and what would prove to be final time. Aron's a big pussy that's afraid of the cancel mob—that's why he's been in hiding. He wholeheartedly agrees with them and thinks a small group of window-lickers should be the lone deciding factor for what people can and can't read. He believes it should all be based on feelings and feelings alone. Either that… or completely the opposite and they can all get fucked.

Printed in Great Britain
by Amazon